As if by Magic

It was just me, then. I was the only person who could see the cat. Which meant that everybody else was going crackers — or I was. Taking a deep, deep breath, I turned slowly back, determined to look that cat squarely in the eyes and ask it what it was doing there, following me. Haunting me. But it was gone.

Jo Furminger

As if by Magic

Illustrated by Alice Englander

Hippo Books
Scholastic Publications Limited
London

Scholastic Publications Ltd.,
10 Earlham Street, London WC2H 9RX, UK

Scholastic Inc.,
730 Broadway, New York, NY 10003, USA

Scholastic Tab Publications Ltd.,
123 Newkirk Road, Richmond Hill,
Ontario L4C 3G5, Canada

Ashton Scholastic Pty. Ltd.,
P O Box 579, Gosford, New South Wales,
Australia

Ashton Scholastic Ltd.,
165 Marua Road, Panmure, Auckland 6,
New Zealand

Text copyright © Jo Furminger, 1989
Illustrations copyright © Alice Englander, 1989

First published 1989

ISBN 0 590 76194 3

Made and printed by Cox and Wyman Ltd.,
Reading, Berks.

Typeset in Baskerville by COLLAGE (Design in Print)
Longfield Hill, Kent.

10 9 8 7 6 5 4 3 2 1

Chapter One

It was the morning after that dreadful storm —
you must remember it. Midsummer's Eve, of
all nights! No rain, but a terrible howling
wind, making you want to burrow down in the
bedclothes and pull them up over your ears.
Clankings and rustlings everywhere, and little
clattering noises on the roof. And afterwards,
things lying around in the garden that hadn't
been there the day before.

Well, I was just setting out for school when
I began to get a really funny feeling. No, it
wasn't a headache or sicky tummy or not
wanting to go or anything like that. It was
weird. It made the back of my neck prickle as if
a spider was walking up underneath my hair.

All right, I know what you're thinking. But
you're wrong. So there. It *wasn't* nits. But it was
definitely scary and, in fact, I stopped. Right
outside our front gate, so you can tell I hadn't

got very far. Suddenly, I looked round with a jump and then I knew what the funny feeling was all about. I was being followed. I *was*. But there was nothing there.

I sort of gulped. And it took a lot of courage not to turn and run straight back into the house yelling for Mum, I can tell you. I could have waited and gone to school with her and Lee who had to be taken to the reception class every morning and brought home every afternoon. But being eight, and in the Juniors, I always went earlier with Laura and Pauline, and there they were, waving to me in the distance and signalling for me to hurry up. So you see, I couldn't turn and bolt back into the house like a frightened rabbit because they'd wonder what was going on.

"Ghosts *don't* come out in the daytime," I said firmly, trying to be convincing but only succeeding in scaring myself even more. There's just something about the actual word "ghosts" spoken out loud, that's enough to make you start looking over your shoulder there and then. Try it and see!

Well, waving back to my friends, I started to

run, but it wasn't any good, the feeling ran along behind me. I was being followed. There wasn't any doubt. But there was *nothing there*.

It stalked me all the way to the school gates. It did. And it crossed over behind us when Mrs Patel led us across the road, brandishing her lollipop, and it followed us into the playground. Correction. Not *us*. Just me. Needless to say, I didn't dare mention this to Pauline or Laura. They'd have laughed like drains. So I just put up with it until the bell went and we all rushed in. I was jolly glad to see that classroom door close behind us, I can tell you!

So you can imagine how I felt when the register was being taken and this horrible, familiar prickling crept up my spine. I nearly answered somebody else's name by mistake. Whatever-it-was had got into the classroom and was watching me. Watching.

The first lesson was story writing, and the title Miss Bold gave us was "Adventure Under The Sea". Well, that sort of thing is easy enough if you're a diver or underwater explorer or submarine commander or whatever, but not so easy when you're sitting in a classroom with twenty-five other people and all you did last summer was paddle your toes in the ocean. And I was just racking my brains for the opening sentence which, as you know, is the most difficult bit, when I looked up. And jumped a mile. Because there was a cat sitting on the table in front of me.

Sea Adventure

It was black all over, except for a tiny white triangle on its chest and a dab of white on the end of its tail. Its eyes were green as marbles, gazing straight at me. And it sat without moving, one front paw firmly on the top of my page.

"Oh!" I gasped out loud. Miss Bold raised her head. She was hearing people read and positively hated interruptions then. So she glared in my direction.

"Did you say something, Natasha?" she asked icily.

"Er . . . er . . . well . . . ," I burbled, thinking, I don't actually need to explain anything now that she's seen the cat. But Miss Bold didn't jump up, or exclaim in amazement, or rush over to shoo it outside. She didn't even look surprised. She just stared at me with a slight frown, waiting for a reply. My mouth kind of froze into the shape of an O, and I began to get an awful, panicky feeling that she couldn't even see the cat. I mean, she was actually looking right *through* it! And when she just said quietly, "Please get on, Natasha, we haven't got all morning," I knew I was right.

Well, as soon as Miss Bold had turned away I nudged Pauline who was sitting next to me, and she looked round with an exasperated frown which said hey, I nearly made a mistake then; and without even twitching, she went back to her story. So with one eye on Miss Bold, so to speak, I peered furtively round the classroom to see if anybody else had noticed the cat. But even Paul the Pincher was getting on with his work for a change. At least, he was sitting stiff as a poker with his nose screwed up and an expression of awful agony on his face which was his way of thinking.

It was just me, then. I was the only person who could see the cat. Which meant that everybody else was going crackers — or *I* was. Taking a deep, deep breath, I turned slowly back, determined to look that cat squarely in the eyes and ask it what it was doing there, following me. *Haunting* me. But it was gone. Not jumped down and run away, because there was nowhere to go. The door was shut, so were most of the windows except one very high up near the ceiling which never closes properly, winter or summer, day or night.

Vanished without trace. I stared down at my book. No quite, though. Right at the top of the page was a muddy little mark. Four tiny spots and a larger one underneath, a cat's paw-print. Weird!

I didn't say anything to Pauline or Laura because before we could get a proper chance to talk, which would have been playtime, something else happened which actually made me forget all about the cat. Half-way through the morning, this new kid came into our class.

Chapter Two

We were about to start our second lesson which was Nature and my *absolute* favourite, except that it was about spiders (yuk!) when the door opened and three people stood there.

One was Mrs Peak the head teacher, one was a rather mousy looking lady and the third was this kid. Well, we all stared, of course, instantly forgetting the spiders. Miss Bold looked up with a smile. She had to, you see, because it was Mrs Peak, even though she hates anybody interrupting her lessons, especially Nature which is her favourite too (I bet she even likes spiders!).

"Good morning!" sang out Miss Bold brightly, and the three people walked into the room. Of course, Mrs Peak strode across as if she owned the place, which I expect most head teachers do really. And the mousy looking lady trailed uncertainly after her, as if she was a bit afraid the floor would suddenly crack under her feet, or turn to jelly, or something. But the third person was the one we all stared at.

She was about the same age as us and so we guessed straight away that she was a new kid come to join the class. But she was *weird*! She wore black, for a start. I mean, can you actually imagine anybody of eight wearing black at school, unless they were dressing up, or maybe putting a bright coloured jumper on top? And although there wasn't a single hole or tear to be seen anywhere in her frock, it just gave the impression of being tatty, and somehow covered with a thin film of dust. It was so long that there was hardly any space between it for legs to show above her socks, which were kind of greyish, not dirty, exactly, just greyish. And her shoes were black, ordinary lace-ups, not even shiny patent leather ones which aren't at all bad, but thick and heavy-looking, with the same kind of dusty air as everything else. Honestly, none of our girls would have been seen dead in them!

"This is Harriet," said Mrs Peak to Miss Bold. And then smiling round the class she

added, "She's staying with her auntie, Mrs Mince."

Of course, we all looked at Mrs Mince and grinned, and even the corner of Miss Bold's mouth snicked up just a little bit. And somebody actually sniggered out loud! Poor Mrs Mince, she kind of shrank into her shoes as if she wished the floor would open and swallow her up.

"Harriet will only be here for a little while," said Mrs Peak. "And I want you to make her feel very much at home."

At home? How could you make anybody feel at home in our classroom? It was just about the worst in the school. With high walls covered in dust where they hadn't been cleaned for *centuries*, and cobwebs in the corners, and massive great iron pipes and radiators all over the place which clanked and groaned when they started warming up or cooling down. And peeling paintwork and a pitted blackboard with half the black worn off. And worst of all, little opaque windows halfway up so that you could only see a bit of the sky if you were lucky. Not to mention the draughts everywhere. The awful thing was that in the spring they came and painted the school in lovely, clean bright colours. But when it was our turn they ran out of money, and just left us like that. So now it wouldn't be done for a month of Sundays. Typical!

"Well, Harriet," said Miss Bold with a big smile. "Who would you like to sit by, I wonder? We have spare seats by Jane Eason, Simon Robbins, Sui Wing, Natasha Brown—"

"Her," said Harriet without hesitation. She pointed straight at me. And I hadn't even put up my hand. Coincidence, right? Maybe she just liked the look of me, or something, because she couldn't have known that I was Natasha Brown of one of the spare seats, could she? Or perhaps it was just a lucky guess. Anyway there she stood with her green, green eyes turned on me, her black hair hanging in lank streaks down to her shoulders, pale face and long, thin nose turned up slightly at the end. Actually, I suppose she was quite pretty in a half-starved sort of way.

"What an excellent choice!" exclaimed Miss Bold enthusiastically. "You *will* look after

Harriet, won't you Natasha dear?"

I nodded speechlessly (well, what else could I do?) while Harriet clumped across the carpet in her frightful shoes and sat down.

"Say goodbye to auntie, now," said Mrs Peak to Harriet.

"Goodbye, auntie," said Harriet obediently. And she sat very still and upright, hands clasped quietly in her lap and eyes cast down. Wow, I thought. I'm supposed to look after *her*? Some fun!

"Now, where were we?" wondered Miss Bold when Mrs Peak had strode out of the room with Mrs Mince scuttling thankfully behind. "Ah yes, spiders!"

Well, we were all enjoying this lesson about spiders, because whatever you think you know already, there's always something else to learn, right? And Miss Bold certainly knew a lot about spiders. Even Harriet sat listening intently, ears positively pricked. When suddenly, Paul the Pincher struck again. He's a truly awful boy whose real name is Paul Phipps, but he has this nasty, spiteful habit of pinching you when you're least expecting it.

The worst time is in Assembly when we have to sit close together on the Hall floor. Somehow he usually manages to end up next to me, even though I do my best to get away from him. And

then, pinch! Just when you're least expecting it.

"Ouch!" I gasped. I really couldn't help it. At the very moment when Miss Bold was coming to a truly gruesome, blood-curdling bit about the spider's eating habits, *pinch*! I glared round in fury.

Miss Bold frowned. "Natasha, please don't interrupt!" she exclaimed. "That's the second time I've had to speak to you this morning!"

Then, before I could open my mouth to complain she added, "And Paul Phipps, just get those hands in your pockets, and keep them there!" She doesn't miss *anything*, our teacher.

So with one of his extra specially stupid grins Paul the Pincher shoved his hands into his pockets and I knew they'd be out again before you could say rabbits, but I'd be ready for him next time. Anyway, he didn't try anything else even when Miss Bold had finished her talk, and I realized it was because his hands were still in his pockets. Just trying to be funny, no doubt.

"Right," said Miss Bold. "Now take out your Nature notebooks and write as much as you can remember about the spider. Harriet, I'll give you a new book in a minute, dear. *Paul Phipps*, get started."

Chapter Three

It was then that we realized there was something peculiar about Paul the Pincher. More than usual, I mean. He was sitting and staring at his grubby knees, and his face was bright red, right to the tips of his extremely large ears. And inside his pockets, a fierce struggle seemed to be taking place.

"Hands out of pockets, now, Paul, and get on," said Miss Bold crisply.

"I can't!" gasped Paul.

Gosh! At that, everybody stopped to listen, ears pricked like mad! If Paul the Pincher, or anybody, thought he could take on Miss Bold and *win*, well . . .

"What?" exclaimed Miss Bold with a frown as black as the inside of a witch's cauldron. Her eyes positively flashed. "Stop being RIDICULOUS, and take your hands out of your pockets!"

"They won't come!" wailed Paul. He pulled and tugged but his hands remained hidden from sight. Miss Bold stared. Her eyes narrowed. Honestly, if a Tyrannosaurus Rex had walked into the classroom just then, it would have turned tail and run!

"What absolute rubbish!" screamed Miss Bold. "Take them out AT ONCE — and get up!"

Well, Paul tried to struggle to his feet with his hands still hidden away. And if you think that's easy, try it and see! For a few minutes he rocked feebly back and forth while we laughed like drains. Honestly, we couldn't help it! And then suddenly he stopped trying, and burst into tears, which only seemed to make Miss Bold more ratty.

"You naughty little boy!" she shouted. "How *dare* you think you can play tricks on me and then pretend to cry? Go and stand by the blackboard THIS MINUTE and DON'T MOVE until playtime, when you can take your work and sit outside Mrs Peak's office to get it finished!" And with that, she grabbed him by his collar and yanked him to his feet.

Well, it served him right. We all knew he could have taken his hands out of his pockets the moment he wanted to. But he'd really gone a bit too far this time!

Seconds later, however, everybody had forgotten all about him because the classroom was silent again and we were ready to start work.

"Now don't forget to write today's date," said Miss Bold. "And the title is simply, 'Spiders'. Then put down everything you know about them."

I picked up my pencil and started to write, and Harriet picked up her pencil and just sat there. Staring at the brand new book Miss Bold had given her.

"Look, open it at the first page," I whispered encouragingly. "Then write the date on the top line, like me."

"I can't!" Harriet whispered back. "I don't know how to work one of these!"

I stared. She was pointing at her *pencil*. I positively goggled. I mean, even babies in the *nursery* know what a pencil is all about.

"You're kidding," I said out loud. Harriet

shook her head.

"Well, look," I said, still feeling that my leg was being pulled a bit. "Just hold it like this — and write!"

"I can't," repeated Harriet. And to prove it, she made a kind of feeble stab at the page leaving a squiggly black mark, while the pencil sort of slid through her fingers and dropped on the floor.

"What is the matter, Natasha?" asked Miss Bold irritably. She was standing at the painting table adding water to powder paints and stirring like mad. Right now she was holding a pot of yellow.

"Please Miss Bold, Harriet can't hold her pencil," I said. "She isn't used to writing with one," I added hastily, not wanting to sound as if I were telling tales.

"What?" exclaimed Miss Bold, her eyebrows arching in amazement. "Harriet, what do you write with at your own school, then?"

She really meant is as a kind of funny, because *everybody* uses pencils, right? That is, unless they're in third or fourth year Juniors or

Comprehensive, which we weren't. Anyway, Harriet started to look round the classroom as if searching for something. By now, everybody was just staring again, and hardly anybody had written a word.

All of a sudden, Harriet's eyes lit on the very thing she wanted, and jumping out of her chair she clumped across to the Nature table. We watched with baited breath as her hand darted down and picked up a feather. Honestly, I'm not kidding. It was from a seagull or pigeon or something, greyish-white and a bit tatty and motheaten, having been kicking around the Nature table for a few weeks.

"My feather," whined Jane Eason sulkily, who had contributed it in the first place. You'd have thought it had come out of *her* wing. Harriet held up the feather.

"I can write with this," she said.

Well, you could have heard a pin drop. The whole class stared from Harriet to Miss Bold, who was staring at Harriet, trying to make up her mind whether Harriet was horribly cheeky or just downright mad — or whether *she* was.

"I see," said Miss Bold at last, in a very

controlled sort of voice. She slammed down the pot of yellow paint and picked up the black, stirring so furiously that little spots flew out in all directions. One of them landed on my book. "Show me how you do it, then."

"Please can I borrow that as well?" asked Harriet politely, pointing to the pot of black paint. At that Miss Bold went bright red. I mean, like a pillar box. Without a word she handed the paint pot to Harriet, and Harriet dipped in the feather, pointed end downwards. And then she began to write.

First the date. Then another dip. Then the title, 'Spiders'. Gosh, her writing was beautiful! For one thing it was all joined up, which we're not allowed to do till the second year. For another, it was so pretty, all little curls and loops and squiggles, like nothing any of us had seen before. Weird!

"Well, Harriet," said Miss Bold in a strangled kind of voice. "I suppose there isn't any point in trying to make you change your handwriting, since you're only going to be with us for a short time. Please carry on."

It was so strange sitting there beside a person writing with black paint and a feather that the people on our table hardly got anything done for *ages* (well, five minutes, anyway) but then we just sort of got used to it, and settled down. When the bell rang for playtime, I had finished my spider story and was pleased to see that Harriet had filled a whole page. She seemed to know even more about spiders than Miss Bold.

Miss Bold had just started to say "Tidy up your tables" which we had to do every time we left the classroom, when there was a great shout from the direction of the blackboard and

Paul the Pincher stood there with his hands in the air, and a great beam of delight on his face.

"They came out!" he yelled. "All by themselves!"

"What a coincidence it should happen at playtime," said Miss Bold sarkily. "Well, you know what you have to do."

Nodding vigorously, Paul leapt across and seized his Nature notebook and pencil, seeming almost happy as he scooted down the corridor towards Mrs Peak's office. Honestly, I've never known him to actually *grin* at the thought of missing playtime before.

Chapter Four

You can always tell who's on duty at playtime by the way the kids behave. Miss Bold is very strict and she always makes us walk nicely into the playground and when the others come peeling round the corner howling like goblins they stop and walk too, knowing they'll get lines, or worse, if they don't. And not one of the boys dares to bring a football to school when Miss Bold is on duty, because she'll confiscate the lot for the rest of the term. Mrs Tranter has been known to do that as well. So has Mrs Blake and Miss Masterton and Ms Crabbe.

But that morning it was Mr White on duty so it was a case of push, shove, jostle and yell, and footballs flying about all over the place. To get away from them you had to lurk in a doorway or hang around the corner of a wall, or dodge behind the trunk of a convenient tree. That was, if you were lucky and managed to get there before a football clonked you on the head.

"Follow me!" I cried to Harriet, and launched forth towards a sycamore tree which wasn't very thick but better than nothing. But before we arrived, Harriet was hit by a football.

It zoomed across and caught her with an awful thump on her cheek, and it was closely followed by seven howling boys who were so busy trying to kick the football away from each other that they didn't even see Harriet. And as for saying sorry, well, is the moon made of green cheese?

"Harriet, come *on*!" I called, panting across to the tree, expecting her to follow. But Harriet just stood there, in the middle of all the boys, an utterly calm look on her face and her cheek turning red where the ball had hit. Oh, gosh, she'll be hurt again in a minute, I thought frantically, and was just about to rush back and get her when a most interesting thing happened. James Pringle, whose football it was, had just drawn back his foot to give it the most enormous kick, when the ball sailed up

into the air and hit him on the nose.

"Ow, ow!" shouted James, clutching his nose which instantly started to bleed.

One of the boys whose name is Something-or-other Earnshaw and is utterly thick, thick, *thick*, didn't even notice, and with an earsplitting whoop he went haring after the ball. But the other five stopped in their tracks, staring at James as if they couldn't quite believe their eyes. Then one of them put an arm round his shoulders and led him towards Mr White, dripping blood all over the place. The others trailed along behind looking rather sheepish, while Earnshaw dribbled away in the distance, toes twirling like a ballet dancer. To find when he got back that there was nobody there.

"Hey, that was really neat!" I said to Harriet, pulling her towards the sycamore tree, because, as I've already said, the air was still thick with flying footballs. "Sort of a freak bounce, right? Couldn't have taught him a better lesson if we'd *wished* for it!" Harriet looked at me from the corners of her green, green eyes, and grinned.

After playtime it was practical Maths with Mrs Samms, who is tall and stiff with short black hair sleeked down over her head in a smooth cap, dark glinting eyes and a long nose which she looks down like a haughty, overgrown elf. And if you don't get things right, well, look out. She's got some really mean, nasty little habits like pulling your hair and tweaking your nose, and kicking your chair and coming up behind you silently and banging the desk very hard with her hand. I've had all of them. Because I can write Nature notes till the cows come home. But ask me to add up two and two and I get five. Every time. Or on a bad day, maybe three. Anyway, you get the idea.

So we waited apprehensively while she bustled importantly around at her desk and then when it was quiet enough to hear a pin drop she raised her eyebrows in the direction of Harriet and said, "And who are you?"

"I'm Harriet," said Harriet. Hands meekly in her lap.

"The girl who writes with a feather," said Mrs Samms. And she gave a disapproving sniff. News had spread round the staffroom, obviously. "Well, while you are in *my* class," said Mrs Samms, looking piercingly at Harriet, "you will use the proper tools." She turned away and addressed the class.

"This morning we are going to make a *perfect cube*. And to do this we need rulers, pencils," (this with a sideways glance at Harriet,) "scissors and paste. Also, a piece of paper like this."

She held one up. "When we have finished measuring, we shall have made a shape which, when glued together, will have six sides, each exactly six centimetres square."

That's how she talked all the time. I'm not kidding. No wonder I could never understand maths!

Turning to the blackboard Mrs Samms showed us how to measure our first line and where to put the dot, which wasn't too bad. I did mine quickly, keeping a careful eye on Harriet in case she needed any help when Mrs Samms wasn't looking. That wasn't as easy as it sounds. Her eyes were everywhere! Especially, it seemed, on Harriet.

"Get your ruler straight, child!" she snapped, circling round the back of Harriet's chair. "And don't you get any ideas about helping her, Natasha Brown!" And she tugged spitefully at one of my plaits. Which was easy because I have about six million of them since I like my hair long and that morning I had a few coloured wooden beads in my fringe to weight the ends down as well. I winced a bit and Harriet saw me. Then she bent over her paper and the next time I looked the dot was in the right place and her pencil was back on the table in front of her. Mrs Samms moved away thank goodness, so I forgot all about Harriet while I painstakingly measured and drew my own shape then cut it out carefully down the lines. Then suddenly, Mrs Samms was back because no sooner had Harriet picked up her scissors than she jerked the back of her chair, making Harriet jump a mile. Then snarling, "Hold them properly, child! Like THIS!" she seized Harriet's fingers, curled them round the scissors none too gently and slammed her hand down towards the paper.

Harriet said nothing. She didn't even flinch,

or turn red. She just stayed absolutely calm. And that seemed to enrage Mrs Samms even more.

"Get on with your work, girl!"she shrieked. "There are some people here who have almost finished glueing their cubes together, and you haven't *even* cut yours out yet!"

Mrs Samms seized Jane Eason's perfect cube and brandished it in front of Harriet's face, turning it this way and that and examining it approvingly through her dark eyes.

"Look at these beautifully sharp lines!" she shrilled, while Jane smirked, smugly. "Her measuring is so wonderfully accurate, and her cutting so careful, and her folding so sharp! This is quite—"

She stopped with her mouth open. Because the next second the beautiful cube was hanging from the end of her chin.

Nobody saw quite how it happened. And for a few moments everybody was taken utterly by surprise. But it didn't take long for somebody to recover enough to titter, which was a signal for all of us to join in and before long the whole class was positively cracking up! Mrs Samms

squinted in horror at the cube hanging from her chin. She put up her hand to pull it gently away, but it wouldn't budge. So she gave it a vigorous yank and it ripped right in half, some sticking to her chin and some to her fingers. Everybody howled.

"Be quiet! SILENCE!" she screamed, and gradually the laughter died down while Mrs Samms struggled to remove the fragmented cube which was now in bits all over her hands.

"My cube! My lovely cube!" wailed Jane Eason, and Mrs Samms whirled round, glaring, the bit of paper quivering from the end of her chin.

"I said, SHUT UP!" she screamed, banging her hand down on the desk. Which was a mistake. Because when she lifted it up again, it was covered with the scraps that Jane had cut away, not to mention Jane's pair of scissors, which now dangled from Mrs Samms' thumb.

"Oh, oh!" gasped Mrs Samms, shaking her hand furiously. Everybody ducked. But we needn't have worried, because the scissors simply didn't move.

"There must be something wrong with this glue!" cried Mrs Samms in horror as she pulled out a handkerchief to wipe the paper from her hands, only to find that it promptly stuck as well.

She barged back to her table, discovering when she got there that eight other cubes and seventeen bits of paper and three pencils had leapt from their places and clung to her skirts as she swept past.

"Children, *don't touch the glue*!" screamed Mrs Samms. "And don't you *dare* get out of your seats while I am washing this off my hands. Somebody, please open the door!"

Seven people leapt to open the door and Mrs Samms swept through, clanking and rustling. And in two minutes she was back, and everything that had been sticking to her was gone.

"They just . . . fell off," she murmured, sinking into her chair. "As soon as I got into the corridor, they simply — fell off! William, will you please go and ask the caretaker to come and sweep up the mess, and to throw away these jars of glue. I *dare not* use them again!"

For the remainder of the lesson, she read us a story, which was a whole lot better than messing around with fiddly paper cubes. But I couldn't help wondering why the glue had affected only her, and none of the rest of us who had used it as well. Even Mrs Samms didn't seem to have noticed that. Weird!

Chapter Five

During the dinner break Harriet stuck to me like glue (if you'll pardon the pun), and I didn't worry too much because I'd got rather attached to her, even though she was a bit oddish. I mean, all she ate for dinner was carrots and parsley sauce. I ask you! But no matter how the dinner ladies tried to coax and tempt her, she wouldn't have anything else.

Anyway, that afternoon when we got back to the classroom — surprise, surprise! There was a message on the blackboard written in white, yellow and red chalk which said, "Invitation to Class 6. Please come to my birthday party this afternoon. From Miss Bold". And up in the corner near the language cupboard, three spare tables had been pushed together and covered with white paper, fringed all round like a tablecloth. And on top of the paper was FOOD! There were twenty-six little plates each having two sandwiches and some crisps and a tiny sausage roll and one chocolate biscuit wrapped in shiny foil. And on Miss Bold's desk was a lovely big square-shaped birthday cake with pink icing all over it and a silver frill round the edge, and one pink candle in the middle.

We all trooped in staring at everything with ooos and ahhhs and little whistles of appreciation. While Miss Bold smiled to herself and went a bit red and pretended to be busy with the register.

"Is it your birthday today, Miss Bold?" called Laura. Miss Bold nodded shyly, and we all chorused "Happy Birthday!" together, and somebody started singing the birthday song so Miss Bold had to sit there until we'd finished, while her smile got wider and wider.

"How old are you?" asked John Kettle. Honestly, he really doesn't know any better. But we stared interestedly at Miss Bold anyway, waiting for her reply.

"Well, actually," said Miss Bold, her eyes twinkling, "I'm as old as my tongue and a little bit older than my teeth."

I ask you! What sort of an answer is that?

While we were trying to work it out she said, "When I've done the register, we'll go out on to the field and I'll read you a story. Then we'll come back inside and have our birthday tea."

So Simon and Helen carried Miss Bold's chair outside and we found a lovely quiet spot in a corner of the field. Most of us chose to sit in the sun — well, we have to make the most of it while we can, right? But Harriet, even though she still sat next to me, managed to wriggle into a little patch of shade cast by a silver birch.

"Now settle down, and I'll begin," said Miss Bold, opening her book. So we all settled down. And it was at that very moment that I saw the cat again. It was under Miss Bold's chair, of all places. Weaving in and out of the legs with its tail in the air and its jade eyes blinking, rubbing round as if purring with pleasure.

My jaw dropped open so far you could have scraped it off the floor with a spoon. Because the cat actually walked right in front of Miss Bold, pressing against her legs — and she never even glanced down! She just went on with the story as if nothing was happening. And what's more, nobody shouted, "Look, there's a cat," or anything like that. So it wasn't long before the horrible truth hit me like a brick. Which was that only I could see it.

Well, thinking I was getting sunstroke or something, I turned to Harriet to signal make way because I'm coming into the shade with you, when I stopped. Because *she* could see the cat as well. It was as plain as the nose on your face. She wore a faint smile and her green eyes were glinting and she was gazing straight at it. Then the cat turned and stared at Harriet and its mouth opened wide in a silent pink miaow. Then it took one step forward as if to run towards her and that was as far as it got. Harriet made a sort of brief movement with one hand, almost like a little wave, as if she was saying "Hi!" to the cat. And when I looked back to see how close it had managed to get to her without anybody noticing still, it had gone. Vanished. There wasn't any cat anywhere at all. Not under Miss Bold's chair, not stepping daintily through rows of sitting children, not scampering away towards the distant hedge. Not streaking back in the direction of the school. Nowhere.

Talk about the jim-jams! This cat business was beginning to get to me. And I really felt that Harriet had something to do with it.

"Was that *your* cat?" I whispered, leaning towards her.

"Natasha BROWN!" came Miss Bold's exasperated voice at once. "Pay *attention*! Honestly, I don't know what's the matter with you today!" She wasn't the only one!

Well, we got back into the classroom eventually and started on our crisps and stuff while Miss Bold rushed round pouring out orange squash or lemonade from big plastic containers. Somehow or other, Harriet's food seemed to disappear, although I never actually caught her chewing. And I was sure that an extra sausage roll appeared on my plate from somewhere. While several other people, including Paul the Pincher ended up with more crisps that they'd started with.

Then, while we were all munching and slurping Miss Bold got a box of matches and lit the sigle pink candle on her birthday cake. And when she blew it out we all shouted, "Make a wish!"

"But don't tell *anybody*," warned Pauline. "Or it won't come true."

We scowled at her. If she hadn't said that, Miss Bold would have said her wish out loud, we were sure. And everybody was *dying* to know.

So Miss Bold blew out the candle and closed her eyes and wished. Silently. And just at that moment I happened to catch sight of Harriet who was sitting bolt upright and absolutely still. Staring at Miss Bold, with her head on one side like a robin. As if actually listening to the wish Miss Bold was making inside her head. Weird!

"Bet you've wished for a boyfriend!" shouted Paul the Pincher with a gross cackle.

"No she hasn't, she's already got one," giggled Samantha.

It was true. I'd seen him. A tall, stringy wimp with steel rimmed glasses and hair down to *here*, meeting her out of school. Probably a violin teacher, or something.

"Lots and lots of money!" screeched Darren Tweddle, as Miss Bold started carving up the cake.

"A new car!"

"A posh dress!"

"A great big remote control colour telly!"

"A video!"

"Two tickets for the cup final!"

"A holiday in Spain!"

"Ugh," said Miss Bold, but we weren't quite sure which one she meant. She looked up and smiled. "Now you're getting quite ridiculous. I haven't wished for anything like that." My guess was that it was something to do with Nature, because Miss Bold enjoys that lesson more than anything. Well, I do too. Except for the life cycle of the silk worm moth, which is the saddest, *saddest* story I've ever heard.

Then she dished out the slices of cake which was the most delicious you have ever tasted, with layers of cream and jam inside, and the pink icing just melted in your mouth like a dream. And after we had cleared away all the crumbs we could draw a portrait of our friend with charcoal. So Laura and Pauline drew each other, and because I'd been landed with Harriet, so to speak, I teamed up with her.

Actually, without meaning to boast, I'm rather good at art and when I'd finished there was a really good likeness of Harriet on my piece of paper, sitting there sort of drooping in her chair, a bit round-shouldered, eyes cast demurely down and hands in her lap. She was a super model because she sat absolutely still till the very last bit. And when I showed her the result, she didn't say a *word*. She just stared, her green eyes unblinking. Well, I hadn't expected her to fall on the ground and kick up her heels in delight, exactly. But she could have said *something*. Even if it was only "Yuk!".

Then Harriet tried to draw me. And it was feeble! Utterly feeble. It was as if she was actually afraid of the charcoal. She stabbed at the paper and made a few faint lines which could have been anything from a dragonfly to an elephant. We were both relieved when the bell went for hometime, I can tell you.

Chapter Six

As we were leaving the classroom, Harriet said,
"Do you think I could come to your house,
Natasha?" That was unexpected, if you like!
But really nice. During the day I'd got rather
attached to her, even though she was a bit
oddish. And I knew my mum wouldn't mind.
Of course, it never occurred to me then that
Harriet wanted anything except my charming
company. Fat chance!

"All right," I said. "But what about your
aunt? Had we better go and tell her first where
you are?"

"No," said Harriet firmly. "She knows I can
take care of myself."

Crumbs!

So we set off down the street, and I tried to
ignore the creepy, tingling feeling down my
back which told me that the cat was following
us. Invisibly. And then, suddenly, "Wooooo!

Waaaaaah! Eeeeee!" There was a hideous screech in front of us and Paul the Pincher leapt out of a gateway.

"Waaaah, hooooo-oo!" he howled, dancing around with his arms in the air, eyes rolling. "I'm the great big nasty bogey-man, coming to get Natasha Brooooown! Woooo!"

"Clear off, you stupid idiot!" I yelled, taking a swing at him with my satchel. Instantly he stopped being a bogeyman and glared.

"I'll *get you* for that," he said nastily. And I knew I'd be in for another pinch, probably during Assembly, right in the middle of Mrs Peak's story. Oh well!

But he had hardly stopped speaking when he began staring upwards and his eyes fairly goggled and I jumped round in case a ghost or something had materialized from under a paving stone, but it wasn't anything like that.

A kite was coming down from the sky. At first it was quite high up so that it looked like a sort of swirling blob of colour against the blue. And then as it got lower we could see that it wasn't just an ordinary four-cornered kite, but one of those shaped like a big bird, with fierce kind of slitty eyes and a big yellow beak painted on the front of it.

"It's broken its string!" shouted Paul the Pincher, pointing excitedly. "Hey, I'm going to catch it and—" He stopped. Staring. In fact, we all did. Because the kite seemed to suddenly hesitate in mid-air, as if it was, well, *looking* for something — or *somebody* — and then it swooped. Just like one of those birds of prey, kestrels, and buzzards, and *real* kites, it dived straight down towards the ground. Towards us. Towards Paul.

We ducked.

"Waaaaaaaaah!" shouted Paul. And he turned and ran. The kite streaked after him. His legs pumped up and down as he hurtled along the road, but the kite kept up with him. And every now and then it actually bumped into his shoulder and around his ears with its painted beak, as if it was trying to peck him. Honestly, I laughed so much that I got the stitch. It was hilarious! And I never even stopped to think just then, how a kite with a broken string could single out one person and chase him along the road.

"Goodbye Paul!" I gurgled, clutching my stomach. "Fancy being afraid of a *kite*."

But he didn't hear me. He was too busy trying to get to Mr Singh's corner shop before the kite ate him all up.

Well, he made it. And as the door closed behind him, the kite tapped against the glass for a moment or two, in that aimless way kites have when there's nobody on the other end of the string. And then all of a sudden it swooped upwards, streaking away like a rocket until it was just a tiny dot in the sky.

Anyway, I was right about Mum. When we got home she took one look at Harriet and you could almost hear her thinking, poor little mite, what she wants is a good few square meals.

"Staying for tea, Harriet honey?" asked Mum, probably already preparing cakes and jellies and such in her mind's eye.

Harriet shook her head, "No thank you, auntie will be expecting me back soon." Strange! All of a sudden, auntie mattered!

"Well, perhaps another day then," beamed Mum kindly.

"Do you want to come up and see my room?" I asked. Harriet nodded. "In a minute, please," she said. "But can we go into the garden first?"

So we went into the garden, and I took my skipping rope just in case. Or maybe Harriet hadn't got a swing at home and wanted a go on mine. Forget it. She hardly glanced at it. And never even noticed the rope twirling invitingly in my hands. Instead, you'll never guess what she did. She walked round the garden, looking at the ground, slowly and thoughtfully, as if inspecting it for worms, or weeds, or something. Weird!

"Lost something, Harriet?" I asked sarkily. I mean, how could she, having only just arrived? She jumped. She really did. As if she'd forgotten I was there!

"Oh, sorry," said Harriet. Then she came up very close and putting her face near mine she whispered, "Can you keep a secret?"

"Of course!" I said instantly. I love secrets — especially other people's. "What is it?"

"I *have* lost something," said Harriet and hesitated as if wondering whether to say any more. As well she might! Then, "A wand," she finished in a rush.

"Wand?" I echoed dimly. How could I ever give away a secret like that? If I told anybody they'd think I was crackers!

"I *know* it fell down here," said Harriet, looking all round. She gazed upwards. "That's the roof and that's the chimney, and that's the big oak tree we—"

"Oh," I smiled, and the penny suddenly dropped. It all made sense. She'd been climbing the old oak tree outside the front of our house and was waving this wand about pretending to be a fairy when the thing shot out of her hand and landed on our roof. That's what I thought, anyway.

"Whew," I said. "You must have been really high up to do that."

"Yes, we were," said Harriet.

I wasn't listening properly, having started to look for the wand by then, or I might have asked her who she was with at the time. But no matter how we scoured the garden, there was no sign of a little stick with a silver star on the end anywhere.

"Can't you get another one from the shop?" I asked Harriet.

She gave me a funny look and said, "Would you like to show me your room, now?"

As we trailed upstairs, Mum popped her head out of the kitchen and called, "Tea in about ten minutes, Tasha!"

Well, okay, you can get in an awful lot of games in ten minutes if you put your mind to it, but Harriet simply didn't want to know. She spent the whole time prying silently around my room, picking things up and looking underneath, intent on finding this stupid wand. As if I was actually *hiding* it from her. I felt pretty cross, I can tell you.

"Look, how about if we make you another wand," I said at last, irritably. I couldn't help it. "I've got some silver paper here, and my dad has some sticks in the shed—"

I stopped. Because Harriet turned and froze me to the spot with a flash of her green eyes, and the room suddenly darkened, as if a cloud had passed over the sun.

Chapter Seven

I'm sure I wasn't imagining it. Because when Harriet looked away with a sigh, I felt myself go limp. Limp as an uncooked sausage.

"It is here somewhere," said Harriet. "I sensed it when we came upstairs." Her nose was positively twitching, like a hound after a scent.

"Look, I haven't got your wand!" I exclaimed angrily. "Don't you think I'd *know* if I had found something like that in our garden?"

"Probably not," said Harriet mysteriously. "Did you hear that wind last night?"

"Could hardly have missed hearing it," I said. It had been fierce enough to blow the old owl right off his perch. And Piers had even rushed out into the garden before breakfast to make sure the chimney was still there.

"I was out in that," said Harriet. "Me and

my mother and Flinders."

"Flinders?" I echoed blankly.

"Our cat," said Harriet.

I stared. Not realizing till ever so much later that my mouth was open.

"Last night was Midsummer's Night," said Harriet. "The darkest, windiest Midsummer's Night for three hundred and seventy-eight years. And we flew across the roof of your house."

I tried to speak, but all that came out was a sort of dry choke.

"My mother dropped her wand," said Harriet. "In fact, the sudden strongest gust of wind snatched it out of her hand and it fell. Right on to yur roof."

My throat untied itself and I managed to croak "*Flew*?"

"On our broomstick," said Harriet. "We're witches. Hadn't you guessed?"

Well, of course I had! I mean, witches come to school every day pretending to be new children, right?

"Harriet," I said at last. "Either you're batty, or I'm cracking up."

"No," said Harriet in a rush. "It's the truth. You must have heard it clatter down. So we sent Flinders to follow you and find out where you went to school. Then we made Mrs Primrose Mince, who is a distant sort of cousin married to a mortal and very feeble, take me there so that I could get into your class and make friends with you. And come home with you to find my mother's wand."

Honestly, I didn't know whether to laugh or

scream. What a story! Anyway, I decided to go along with it for a bit and said in the calmest voice I could manage, "So you're a witch, then?"

"Yes," said Harriet. Quite seriously. Utterly straightfaced. "My mum is *very* powerful, of course. And I can do a little bit, like the things that happened at school today—"

"What?" I said.

"You know, with Paul the Pincher," said Harriet. "And Mrs Samms. And the football."

The fearful little storyteller! "You must have found it very difficult, without your wand, I mean," I said coldly.

"Oh no, not simple things like that," said Harriet. "Please try to think, Natasha. I know it's here somewhere. In this house!"

"You're right up a gum tree there, Harriet," I said cheerfully. "The only thing we found in our garden after the storm, apart from a lot of broken twigs, was an interesting piece of driftwood."

Harriet stiffened. You could almost hear her brains whirring round like cogs in a wheel. "Was it about this long?" she hissed, measuring with her hands. "And a bit bent in the middle, like a dog's hind leg? And a sort of yellowish-gold colour?"

I nodded. Amazed, actually, if you want the truth. I mean, how could she *know* that Piers had found it, and my dad said it was a lovely piece of polished yew, not the kind of wood you'd find hereabouts.

"Where is it?" She seemed suddenly to have grown taller, and to be almost towering over me with a menacing frown. Imagination, right? Even so I said in a voice which quivered a bit, "I guess it's in Piers' room. He said he was going to . . . to . . . carve a seal out of it."

"No!"

Before I could stop her Harriet streaked out of my room on to the landing and actually had her hand on Piers' door ready to push it open before I got there.

"Harriet, stop!" I cried. "He'll *kill* me if I touch anything!"

And at that very moment, my big macho brother who is fourteen and goes to the Comp, came pounding up the stairs.

"Hey, Tash, get away from my door! And

take your trespassing friend with you!" he bellowed.

"We weren't going in, honest, Piers," I said in what I hoped was a soothingly reassuring tone.

"Huh, didn't look like it," said Piers, glaring at Harriet.

"My friend has lost a . . . a . . . wand," I said. "And she thought it might be in your room."

I felt really daft saying it. Especially when Piers grinned down from somewhere up near the ceiling and said, "Now, do I look like the sort of person who'd play with a wand? Get lost, both of you!" And he stood with his back firmly against the door.

Harriet said nothing. But her green eyes seemed to glow on that dim landing, like a cat's.

"Wait, w-w-wait!" I stammered, sensing trouble. I clutched Harriet's arm. "Piers, we did find something after the storm last night. Remember?"

"What, that piece of wood?" said Piers, staring. "You mean, that old piece of wood?" He looked from one to the other of us as if we'd

both gone mad.

"You see?" I almost screeched. "It's *hers*! Piers, you've got to give it back!"

He said, "That's a *wand*? You're kidding me! It's just an old piece of driftwood, blown into the garden by the storm. I'm going to carve a seal out of it!"

Harriet stiffened. "You mustn't do that!" she said. "The wand will protect itself!"

I had the sudden awful vision of Piers picking up his knife and being instantly turned into a frog. Or worse. Because up there, in the gloom of the landing, she didn't sound like a girl any more. Her voice was cold and piercing as an icicle. I found myself actually starting to shake. Like sickening for the 'flu.

"Piers—"

"This is absolute *crackers*!" burst out Piers angrily. Only he didn't say "crackers". He said a word we're never, *ever* allowed to say in our house. He glared down from Harriet to me and back again with a big, dark frown. "Little girls' games, huh? Okay then, there's your rotten wood! Go and get it!"

And with that he threw open his bedroom

door and stomped furiously down the stairs. It was awful! I wanted to cry, I really did.

So there it was, the polished piece of driftwood. Resting on Piers' desk under the window, gleaming in a ray of afternoon sunlight. Harriet clumped across the room and picked up her wand, stroking it lovingly with her fingers, just like Piers when he thought he was going to carve it into a seal.

And now the crisis was over, I felt very miffed with her. Because Harriet was gazing down at that scrap of old wood as if it was made of pure gold and encrusted with precious stones. You'd have thought she'd just found the Crown Jewels dumped in a dustbin.

"Piers was really keen on that," I said at last, a bit of a cutting edge to my voice. "I hope you're satisfied."

"I'll make it up to him, I promise," said Harriet. I didn't believe her. Because I didn't know how she could, and what's more, didn't really care.

"You don't believe me, do you?" said Harriet.

"No I don't," I said bluntly. Might as well

tell the truth, right? "If you want to know, I think you're just a nasty, spiteful girl and quite an ordinary person, and that all those things that happened at school could be explained in a perfectly *ordinary* way."

Even the cat, I thought. My grandmother always said that if a cat doesn't want to be seen, it won't. Okay, it *was* queer how she'd known about the driftwood, but so what? Maybe she'd been sitting in the tree spying down at our garden when Piers had picked it up. Maybe she was in the window of a nearby house with a telescope trained on Piers' room. Maybe anything. Anything but a witch.

"Look, I've got to go and have my tea now," I said grumpily.

Harriet followed me down the stairs and I opened the front door. I didn't even offer to walk part of the way home with her. A witch who's got a magic wand can take care of herself. Right? There was a sudden movement outside and there on the garden wall was the black cat, waiting for Harriet and rubbing around the gatepost, tail in the air.

"See you at school in the morning, then," I

said in an offhand sort of way.

"No you won't," said Harriet. "I don't need to come any more."

She grinned. (Did I ever mention that her teeth were, well, just a little bit *pointed* . . . ?)

"Look," said Harriet. "You're my friend, and I really want you to believe me. So tomorrow morning, ask Miss Bold if the spotted flycatchers are nesting in her creeper now. That was her birthday wish, you know."

I stared.

"And," she went on, "when you get to school, you'll find something else, especially for you. Something you never mentioned to anybody. Something you never thought could happen in a month of Sundays. A sort of little goodbye present from me."

There was a sudden movement in the bushes nearby but when I looked, there was nothing there. And when I turned back to speak to Harriet, she had gone.

Chapter Eight

Well, the first odd thing that happened after that was that I got back into the house and saw Piers sitting at the table with Harriet's wand in his hand.

"Where . . . where —" I began, and Piers said, "Your weirdo little friend changed her mind after all, then. Left her precious *wand*, or whatever it is, on my desk." And picking up his knife he made the first little nick in the wood. I held my breath. But nothing happened, because it *wasn't* Harriet's wand. Couldn't have been. She'd been holding that in her hand right up to the moment she'd disappeared.

So you can probably guess I was in rather a tizzy till the time came to go to school next morning. And for once I could hardly wait to get there. The second I was out of the house you couldn't see my heels for dust. Laura and

Pauline were there as usual and I just whizzed past them like an Olympic sprinter panting, "Got to get there early this morning!" Leaving them to trundle behind with expressions of amazement.

On the way across the playground I caught up with Miss Bold as she strode towards our classroom. And in my mind's eye was a picture of Harriet. Harriet watching Miss Bold blow out her one pink candle. Harriet with her head on one side, listening to Miss Bold's secret thoughts.

"Did — did your birthday wish come true

yet, Miss Bold?" I wheezed, putting on the brakes.

"Oh! My birthday wish? Oh, Natasha, that was the most extraordinary thing."

Wait for it, I thought. Miss Bold went on, "For years and years I've been hearing a pair of spotted flycatchers in the trees around my garden. Squeaking away to each other like mad, the moment they arrived back in our country! And I've been longing to see them, but I never had. Not even a tiny glimpse. So I wished on my candle that I could see a spotted flycatcher. And can you believe it?"

I couldn't resist it. I couldn't. "When you looked out of your window this morning, a pair of spotted flycatchers had started to build a nest in the creeper," I said.

Miss Bold stared down at me, astonished. Then she laughed. "What a clever guess, Natasha! That's exactly right!"

By now we had reached the classroom and Miss Bold fumbled in her bag for the key. Then she threw open the door and stopped with one foot in the air. Stunned. Because Harriet had done it. Harriet had waved her wand somewhere and made *my* wish come true. Harriet had read my mind and painted our grotty old classroom just the way I had imagined it. And a little bit more.

It was *wonderful*! The walls were a delicate shade of apricot and the doors were the colour of melon peel and the ceiling like vanilla ice cream. She had replaced the old pitted blackboard with a smooth new one and put in sparkling windows that we could see through to the trees and fields beyond. And she had filled the room with polished wooden furniture and in place of the chipped enamel sink was one of shiny stainless steel. And on Miss Bold's new table was a huge bunch of cream and apricot roses in a glinting crystal vase.

"Oh, Natasha, this is *fantastic*!" cried Miss Bold, gazing round. "Yesterday we were bottom of the list, and now, just look! They must have changed their minds suddenly. And they must have worked all night to have finished by this morning! Oh, I must go and ask Mrs Peak to ring the office and thank them!"

She bustled away, beaming. And you won't

be a bit surprised to hear that Mrs Peak didn't know a thing about it either. She rang the office and two men came out and did a lot of staring around and mumbling between themselves. And there was a fearful hoo-ha in the end because nobody had given any of the painters a work-sheet to say it had got to be done. Eventually they left after a lot of huffing and puffing. Because once a place has been painted, they couldn't very well scrape it all off and make it manky again, could they?

Well, Miss Bold was in a really good mood for the rest of that day. And at playtime I went and stood under the sycamore so that nobody else would hear me whisper, "Thanks, Harriet. I do believe you now," into thin air. And I knew for certain that she wouldn't be coming to school again. All I had left to remind me of my strange friend was a charcoal drawing. Only the funny thing was that when Miss Bold came to pin them up later that day on our brand new apricot-coloured pin-boards, mine somehow seemed to have disappeared. The piece of paper was there with my name on, but the drawing of Harriet had vanished.

"That's strange," said Miss Bold, waving it in the air and frowning. "Are you sure you did one, Natasha?" I didn't actually answer. I mean, what was the point? But picture or no, I knew I would *never*, ever forget the magical day when Harriet came.